Lost &

by

Christie Capps

A Pride & Prejudice Novella

Timeless Romance for the Busy Reader

For information on new Christie Capps releases and other news, please sign up for my newsletter at: jdawnking.com

Christie Capps is a pen name for Joy King, who also writes as J Dawn King.

She can be contacted on social media at:

Facebook: www.facebook.com/JDawnKing

Twitter: @JDawnKing

Email: jdawnking@gmail.com

One

DARCY

Fitzwilliam Darcy could not keep his mind from wandering. Each spring when he traveled to Rosings Park in Kent, his exposure to the mundane topics and outlandish opinions of his aunt Lady Catherine de Bourgh bored him almost to tears. This year was no exception.

As the subject matter of her latest discourse changed from table linens to planting potatoes, Darcy glanced about the room to see how the other occupants fared.

His cousin Anne, the only child of Lady Catherine, sat quietly next to her mother. Rarely did she look up from where her hands were clasped tightly in her lap. Occasionally, his cousin's companion would inquire as to her health. Not one word was exchanged as Anne either nodded or shook her head.

From his youth, Darcy had not been able to imagine a worse fate than to be the child of the mistress of Rosings Park. Prior to the loss of her father when she was ten years of age, there had been occasional spurts of gaiety in the house during Darcy's annual stay at the estate. Since then, he could recall none.

Instead, each day passed with stifling regularity. Lady Catherine enjoyed nothing more than to hold court in her garishly decorated drawing room. Her guests were expected to enjoy each day's performance.

Colonel Richard Fitzwilliam, the second son of Lady Catherine's brother, was his favorite relative. He had left Rosings earlier that morning to see to repairs needed on two of the cottages occupied by his aunt's tenants.

If only Darcy had thought to make the same excuse. He could have been gone from the tedium inflicted by his aunt.

Darcy had no doubt Richard's quick mind would conjure up delightful jokes at the expense of his aunt when the two men later earned the privacy of the library. They would laugh, then shamefully admit it was bad form to make a mockery of the imperious Lady Catherine de Bourgh in her own house. Darcy would have no lingering regrets and he was confident Richard would feel the same.

His aunt's sycophantic parson, Mr. Collins, was accompanied this day by his wife, his wife's young sister, and a guest in their home, a young lady who had completely unsettled him when he had earlier visited Hertfordshire, Miss Elizabeth Bennet. Miss Elizabeth was…she was…argh! He would think of her no more.

Mrs. Collins, the former Miss Charlotte Lucas, hailed from a small farming village called Meryton. Prior to her recent marriage, she was often in company with her neighbor and friend, Miss Elizabeth.

His aunt now expounded on the vitally important topic of dairy cow management. Darcy shook his head slightly enough not to gain notice. His aunt had no dairy herd on her estate, so why she deemed herself an authority puzzled him exceedingly.

Darcy surveyed the two friends, deciding to admire the one and ignore the other.

Where Mrs. Collins' countenance was calm, Miss Elizabeth's was vibrant. Although she sat still, Darcy could see her eyes flash and knew her mind had wandered as his had done.

Of what was she thinking? Was she imagining all sorts of activities she would currently rather be engaged in than sitting on an uncomfortable sofa listening to the puffed-up opinions of a woman wholly unrelated to her?

Mrs. Collins' brown hair was hidden beneath a hat with one feather sticking up. Miss Elizabeth's rich chocolate locks were pulled back into some sort of a knot at the back of her neck. A few tendrils had escaped their confines when she had removed her bonnet. Darcy was eternally grateful they had broken loose from the pins. One curl draped itself down the right side of her neck. Darcy's fingers itched to put it back into place.

Mrs. Collins' eyes were a…well he was unsure if he ever had noticed their color. Miss Elizabeth's were a stunning blue, the color of the sapphire necklace his mother wore when she sat for the family portrait currently hanging at his estate in Derbyshire, Pemberley. Lady Anne Darcy's eyes had been brown, like his. Miss Elizabeth's were rimmed with thick dark lashes that looked too heavy for a mere mortal female. Like his own dearly departed mother's had done, the young lady's eyes easily revealed their owner's every thought and feeling.

In the month he had stayed in Hertfordshire the autumn prior, Darcy had been exposed to the full range of Miss Elizabeth's emotions. Concern—the time when she had walked three miles from her home of Longbourn to his friend's estate to care for her eldest sister when she was ill. Kindness—as she tenderly saw to Miss Bennet's every need. Humor—when she engaged in playful banter with either himself or his host at Netherfield Park, Charles Bingley. Wit—each time she skillfully avoided Miss Caroline Bingley's jealous barbs and bitter anger.

Darcy quietly sighed at the memory. *So much for ignoring her!*

During the one occasion Miss Elizabeth had accepted his offer for a dance, at a ball Bingley held for the neighborhood, their discourse had rapidly changed from a proper discussion of the weather to a confrontation about his former childhood friend, George Wickham. Her eyes had shot fire at Darcy as she called him to account for his rumored actions against the errant lieutenant.

By the end of the evening, Darcy concluded his care and concern for her had grown to an interest he never before had for an unattached female. He despised himself for his weakness. Her lack of connections and the poor coffers of her family's estate made it a degradation to continue his association. Thus, he ran back to London the next morning, dragging Bingley with him, hoping to put her out of sight and out of his mind.

An impossible dream.

Unexpectedly, he arrived in Kent to find her happily ensconced in her the parsonage. The shock to his senses at seeing her once again had disturbed his equilibrium until the cousin traveling with him, Colonel Richard Fitzwilliam, had noticed.

Denial of any attachment was imperative, or Richard would tease and taunt until Darcy needed to resort to extreme measures. For example, he could banish his cousin from his wine cellar, forcing him to drink weak tea or water when he refused to return to his barracks and stayed at Darcy House. Or, he could have Cook serve beets. Richard detested them.

During the week since their arrival, Darcy made it a game to distract his cousin from turning his unwanted attention towards him. He also determined to effectively hide his interest in Miss Elizabeth—for, in truth, cursedly interested he remained.

His aunt's tone changed, catching his attention.

"I will not be thwarted," Lady Catherine barked. "You shall walk to the folly when next you stroll the grounds, Miss Elizabeth. I will have it no other way."

The folly? Darcy was perplexed. Why should his aunt demand a guest in someone else's house make the four-mile trek to an overgrown monstrosity he and Richard had termed "the tomb"?

"While I thank you for your recommendation, I cannot imagine doing so until the rains cease and the ground dries." Miss Elizabeth's voice, opposite of his aunt's, was light and pleasing.

Like her figure.

He swallowed.

"Upon my word," said her ladyship, "you give your opinion very decidedly for so young a person. What is your age?"

"I am not yet one and twenty," Miss Elizabeth admitted with a slight smile.

Again, Darcy wondered at her imagination. Was she seeing his aunt as a matron of elevated rank? Somehow, Darcy thought not.

"Does Colonel Fitzwilliam travel in this weather, or do you think he was able to find shelter?" the young lady inquired.

Why was Miss Elizabeth asking about the colonel? Jealousy speared him in the heart. If Darcy could not wed her, surely neither could Richard. As the second son of an earl, he needed to see to his fortune. The portion the five Bennet daughters shared was meager. It would never do.

But, was she attracted to his cousin? Richard Malcolm Fitzwilliam was the best man he knew. Loyal, courageous, and amiable, the colonel was a manly person of many skills. He could navigate a battlefield as easily as he did a ballroom.

"My nephew has withstood more than a little sprinkle of rain." Lady Catherine lifted her nose until her chin pointed directly at Miss Elizabeth. In Darcy's opinion, it was not her most attractive pose. "He cares for nothing more than seeing to the needs of my tenants. No sacrifice is too large for the colonel. As a matter of record, both my nephews are devoted to me. In particular, Darcy's attachment to Anne is most admirable."

He now found himself the recipient of Lady Catherine's focus.

"My sister's fondest wish was for the marriage of our children to join our two estates into one ownership that would set the Darcy name equal to the Cavendish's." Lady Catherine continued, much to his chagrin. She addressed no one in particular. "Anne was named for my sister. My daughter was born for the role of mistress of a grand estate. Pemberley will do."

At her mother's comment, the daughter barely showed a reaction.

Darcy knew Anne's poor health would never permit her to do anything other than her current activities. For years, when they had a few moments of private conversation, Anne had expressed her desire to remain at Rosings. She had no interest in relocating to Derbyshire, in marriage, or in bearing his heir.

Darcy shuddered at the thought. He loved his cousin as he did all of his family. But marry Anne? Take her to his bed to create a child? Ugh! Never.

His aunt's voice interrupted his pondering, and for once he was grateful.

"I do believe Mr. and Mrs. Collins and their guests shall not have too much difficulty strolling back to the parsonage. I am conscious of all matters pertaining to the care of those under my influence. They shall not suffer from the exercise."

Darcy's mouth dropped open. He was appalled at her comment. Where she would not deign to step outside in the inclement weather, her guests would be turned out for a good soaking? Rivulets of rain streaked down the windows of the drawing room as a brisk wind whipped branches from nearby shrubs into a tangle.

His aunt was preposterous! The little conversation he had shared with Mr. Collins, while in Hertfordshire, found the parson bragging about how often his aunt had made her carriage available to him. Apparently, he had overstated the situation to elevate his own importance.

Darcy would order his own carriage be prepared when the party from the parsonage returned to their cottage. Good manners, which should have come with his aunt's privileged upbringing, would not permit anything less.

Glancing at Miss Elizabeth, he noted her struggles. Surreptitiously wiping a tear from the corner of her eye with one hand, she pressed the other ever tighter over her lips. The poor girl was attempting to control her mirth.

The gleam in her eyes danced. She was everything lovely.

Hoping to provide relief, he offered, "Have Miss Elizabeth and Miss Lucas been shown your library, Aunt?"

"My library," Aunt Catherine mused. "I do not believe so."

"Then I would be pleased to direct them." He started to stand when, most unexpectedly, Anne rose to her feet.

"That will not be necessary, Darcy," his cousin spoke at almost a whisper, as if the effort to talk was more than she could bear. "I shall retire from company and can show the ladies the room. It is barely out of my way."

Before he could reply, saving himself from expressing his disappointment, his aunt spoke, "I cannot imagine Mrs. Collins' sister has much interest in reading when she can learn far more in my presence. She may remain here." Lady Catherine loved an audience, so the idea of being deprived of one attentive listener was apparently unpalatable. "You may take Miss Elizabeth, Anne. I see little interest on her part in the smooth running of a household. She will suffer for it, I tell you."

With grace, the lovely parsonage guest stood to walk from the room with Anne.

The light dimmed. Not literally, of course. A multitude of candles burned around Lady Catherine's throne-like chair, keeping the rest of the room in shadows.

A sour taste erupted in his mouth when he considered the decision confronting him. He needed to either end his struggle by letting Miss Elizabeth go or offer for her before much more time passed. This vacillation was unlike him.

Darcy knew his reputation of being reticent in company and having little tolerance for society. She, on the other hand, pleasantly moved from person to person, encouraging their joy and seeing to their comfort. Miss Elizabeth was as at ease in a gathering as was Richard or Darcy's other close friend, Charles Bingley.

She would complete him.

Stunned, Darcy's realization that he needed her, not just wanted her, jolted him. When he stood to bow the ladies out of the room, his eyes would not leave Miss Elizabeth.

How could he not have seen it before? She was perfection. Surely, her impertinence, her almost non-existent dowry, and her healthy zest for living would be found by some to be less appealing. However, he found her appealing on every level.

He, Fitzwilliam Darcy, prey to fortune-hunting mothers with their insipid daughters, had fallen irreparably in love with Miss Elizabeth Bennet.

How could this be? He had gone from repudiation to agreement in the time it had taken him to watch her walk from the room.

Was this the impulse of a moment? He could not recall a time when a decision had hit him with the power of a mountain falling upon him like this one had done. With his next breath, he knew…he knew his life was forever altered.

Dazed, he was unaware of the conversation surrounding him. When his aunt loudly commanded all remaining in the room to look at the clock, Darcy obeyed.

Thirty minutes? She had already been in the library a half hour?

"Mr. Collins, pull the cord to summon Smyth," his aunt insisted. "Miss Bennet needs to come back to the drawing room. Our guests can, then, remove themselves to their own house. I have a private matter to discuss with Darcy before Richard returns."

Did his aunt's rudeness have no limits? Apparently not.

Shaking his head at the embarrassment of having such a relative, he missed the butler reentering the room after his summons.

"I am sorry to say, Lady Catherine, that the young lady is no longer in the library. The footman on duty, who is constantly vigilant, states that while she entered the room, she did not leave."

"How can this be?" his aunt proclaimed as Darcy jumped to his feet. "Impossible!"

"What has my cousin done now?" from Mr. Collins, who immediately moved to Lady Catherine's side.

"Oh, no!" from Mrs. Collins and her sister, both wearing their deep concern like an outer garment.

Darcy ran from the room, down the hallway, to the library. Entering, he hoped to see Miss Elizabeth seated comfortably on the sofa in front of the burning fireplace, a book in her hand and a smile upon her face. Instead, he looked from one end of the room to the other. Empty.

Checking the two windows and the French doors tucked between shelf-lined walls, Darcy found them firmly locked from the inside. Miss Elizabeth could not have used either avenues for departure.

"How could she vanish into thin air? She is certainly not here," he mused.

The pounding of Darcy's heart shot to a speed unknown by him. Worry filled him as his mind raced.

Pemberley had three hidden shortcuts leading from one room to another. Might not Rosings have the same?

Going to the wall panel next to the fireplace, he pounded on the surface with his fist, yelling, "Miss Elizabeth!"

He waited. Nothing.

Moving further down the wall, he repeated his actions. Again, nothing.

By then, Smyth, apparently discerning his intent, was rounding the room in the other direction doing the same. On a signal from Darcy, they both rattled the walls with their tightly-clenched extremities. Nothing.

"Do you trust the footman?" Darcy asked the aging butler.

"With my life," the man answered with no hesitation.

Then, she was gone—disappeared without a trace.

Darcy's stomach sank to his toes. They needed to find Miss Elizabeth, and they needed to find her now.

Two

DARCY

"Secret passages? Of what are you speaking, Nephew?" His aunt stood and approached him. "As mistress of Rosings Park, I know every inch of this house, inside and out. Had there been hidden hallways from one room to the next, I would be aware," she insisted. Fluttering her hand, she waved off his concerns. "No, Mr. Collins' cousin has rudely run off to the parsonage with no intentions of thanking me for my hospitality. Young people these days!"

"She would never…" Darcy growled. His breath would be wasted defending Miss Elizabeth. There was nothing he could say his aunt would believe.

"I shall dismiss the footman immediately for his inattention." His aunt was known for intolerance. "Miss Elizabeth has undoubtedly left Rosings, walking right by him, with no care to giving consideration to her hostess for my condescension." Turning to her remaining guests, she insisted, "You may leave for the parsonage. When you come upon your guest, feel free to inform her I will no longer welcome her into my presence. She means nothing to me."

As Mr. Collins sputtered his apology for the presumed slight given by his cousin's daughter, Mrs. Collins approached Darcy.

"You will search until you find her?" she whispered. "Lizzy is not the sort to run off as your aunt stated. I fear she has come to harm."

Darcy feared the same.

Reassuring the woman, he tasked Smyth with sending a rider to find the colonel. Richard would be the best man to find the missing young lady. When they were children, no matter how diligent Darcy was in finding a proper hiding place, Richard seemed to hunt him down with ease. It had been one of his life's greatest frustrations before they outgrew the game.

The rest of Rosings' staff were divided so every floor of the grandiose building was searched. A few of the grooms volunteered to look outside the doors and windows for evidence of her dainty footprints, a great sacrifice in the heavy downpour.

With a nod from the butler, they were gone. Leaving Lady Catherine standing alone in the middle of the room, Darcy gave her no further thought. Returning to the library, he stood at the room's doorway to peer inside. Slowly scanning from one wall to the next, he finally noted something distinctly out of place. A narrow section of shelves was lined with cobwebs and dust-covered books to the point they appeared filthy and damaged. The wood holding up the books was dull in appearance, in direct contrast to the surrounding bookcases, which gleamed from having wax rubbed into the surface then polished out.

As he cautiously approached, Darcy noted an oddity he had never noticed before. The floor, thick with dirt and grime, had a circular seam in front of it which apparently ran behind the wall. The whole area in close proximity smelled of mildew and damp.

What is this?

Without hesitation, he stepped on the surface, placing footprints on a area that appeared to have not been disturbed in decades and started pulling books from the shelves. His uncle Sir Lewis had been short of stature, so Darcy began with the shelf at chest height. He was only three books in when he heard the click and felt movement below him. Before he could step aside, the bookcase, floor, and himself quickly spun into a dark void. The latch closing behind him when the wall came to a stop was deafening in the silence.

His rising panic was overridden by his need to find her. He hated the darkness.

"Help me." The distant sound of her voice was a relief. "Help me. I am here."

Fear for her drove him forward. Extending his arms, he easily touched both walls of the passageway. Running his hands through the dust and debris, his right foot unexpectedly hit the front of the first step of a staircase. Unable to stop his momentum, he crashed forward, the edge of the third stair banging into his knee. The pain was nothing to him.

Scampering to his feet, he again reached out for the walls.

Move forward. Find her. Move forward. Help her.

"Help!"

She must have heard his fall.

Rushing up the stairs, he pulled his hands from the walls. Instead, he held them in front of him feeling each upcoming tread, so he knew when he reached the top. Carefully, but quickly, he passed down a short landing only to reach another set of stairs. Climbing as rapidly as possible in the pitch blackness, Darcy gave no heed to hanging webs or the dirt now covering his face, hands, and clothing.

"Elizabeth!" His voice reverberated down the narrow passage. "Where are you?"

"I am here." The muffled tone was clearer. He was getting closer. "Help me, please."

The wall hit him square in the face while he was distracted by her voice.

"Oof!" Stepping back, his hands roamed the surface. The wood extended only to his right. He had reached the back corner of the house.

"Elizabeth," he yelled again.

"You are closer. I hear you better."

Taking six steps, he reached another wall. Pounding on the surface, he was thrilled when she immediately pounded back.

Her direction was clear. "There is a latch to the right of the door on the casing. It is a small button." Her anticipation of rescue warmed him.

His fingers easily found the indentation. He pressed the small nob and the door at the same time. Within seconds he was inside, allowing the door to slam behind him.

"No!" Her despair sent chills down his spine. "No! No! No!" she cried as she roughly pushed him aside to reach behind him.

"What?" He could not see her but felt each rap of her fist on the wood with every beat of his heart.

"We are stuck, Mr. Darcy." Her disappointment bordered on grief. "I have found no means of reopening either the door we came through or the one in front of us."

Of all things, Darcy wished for light. Why had he not grabbed a candle or two? He was a fool.

Feeling the walls, he measured the enclosure to be the size of a small wardrobe. Panic at their situation had been planted when he had first entered the passageway downstairs. It had budded when he hit the first set of stairs. With each step into the darkness, Darcy's anxiety had grown. Now that he was in a small room no larger than a closet, he felt it blooming until it became a living, breathing entity.

The air sucked from his lungs. He hated small spaces. What he loathed even more were small, *dark* places, such as the one they currently occupied.

Beads of moisture gathered on his upper lip and at his hairline. He could feel dampness on his palms. Darcy had no doubt what would happen next—full-blown hysteria as the walls pressed in upon him.

Pulling to loosen his cravat, his elbows paid no attention to whom and what they hit. When Miss Elizabeth exclaimed, the fact that he had personally caused her harm barely registered.

He needed to breathe.

The stupid knot would not loosen. He would terminate Thornton's employment as soon as he…removed…the…blasted…cravat.

His hands shook. His stomach roiled. Giving up on his neckwear he, instead, pounded his hands on the door through which he had come. Turning, he pushed his weight against what had to be their escape route. Then, when he felt not a budge, he covered his face with his hands and, sliding down the back wall, he sank to the floor.

Kicking out, his boot heels crashed into the wood. If his arms could not move the door, his powerfully muscled legs surely would see them released. Nothing moved. Nothing broke. Nothing.

His despair was complete.

"Mr. Darcy." From a distance he heard her. From a great distance. "Mr. Darcy!"

Intellectually, he knew she was no more than a few inches away within the space of the room. Yet, his mind was in a distant time and place where he could not be reached.

"Breathe," she demanded. "If you do not, I will slap your face."

If only he could do as she asked. He yearned for the relief full lungs would provide.

Despite hearing her words, the first blow was unexpected. The second one was not. Her grabbing his shoulders and shaking merely served to irritate him.

Banging his head against the heavy wood, he yelled, "Leave off!"

Then, a reprieve. Pure, comforting succor.

Her small hands cupped his own. Starting where his sleeve ended, she softly stroked down the back of his fingers, speaking soft words to soothe him.

"Look, Mr. Darcy. There is a small ribbon of light under the door behind me. Do you see it? Imagine all the oxygen and hydrogen atoms floating our way. Open your eyes and see the sweet abundance of air flowing up into your nostrils." She continued her chant. "Do you not see the possibilities? Why, we are covered in wonderful, refreshing air. The same air we get irritated with as we walk the countryside trying to keep our bonnets in place." She chuckled. "I refer, of course, to *ladies* with their bonnets strolling the lanes around our homes. Although, I can imagine it a task to keep your tall beaver on your own head when you race over the meadows with the wind in your face. Can you now feel it? Is the air hitting your cheeks and forcing its way into your mouth as you revel in the enjoyment of your horse's pace?"

He felt it. A momentary wisp that grew to cover his mouth and nose.

She had blown into his face.

Hesitantly, as if it would disappear if he moved, he breathed in. When his efforts were successful, he again inhaled. He did so four times in a row before his mind registered his conquest of the situation. Pausing, holding his air to himself, he thought to try again. Four more times he both inhaled and exhaled.

As he did so, her hands clasped his own, absorbing his fears.

"Pray, open your eyes enough to see the light, sir. You will have no regret for I imagine the distance between the floor and the edge of the door to be above half inch." She tugged at his fingers. "Am I correct in my estimation, Mr. Darcy?"

She moved her hand to his chest, surely feeling the pounding of his heart.

"Mr. Darcy, do not forget the sheer magnitude of air drifting up from that massive gap." She patted the chest pocket of his coat. Her hand burned all the way to his skin. "Now, look. Pray open your eyes. You will have no regrets, I promise."

In his memory, which now seemed somewhat operational, she had never asked him for anything. He could do this for her. He *would* do this for her.

Barely cracking his lids open, he spotted the light—a thin strip of hope. The intensity of his relief was immense, releasing most of the pressure from his chest and stopping his hands from shaking.

In the way of men, awkwardness at having his personal weakness displayed for the woman he adored to see almost paralyzed him to the same extent his panic at finding himself in a small, dark space had done.

Whatever would she think of him now?

Three

ELIZABETH

Mr. Darcy had, since the moment she first laid eyes upon him at the Meryton assembly six months past, left the impression with her and her neighbors that he was unbending. Stiff. Unyielding. Never could she have thought him to display a weakness like every other man of her acquaintance.

John Lucas, Charlotte's only brother, had an inclination for drink. Under normal situations when he was away from the tavern, he was a pleasant enough fellow. When he drank? He bullied others more vulnerable than he. It was an ugly aspect and an affront to any good woman.

Mr. Bingley, temporary proprietor of Netherfield Park, had displayed a lack of firmness as he gave in to the demands of his selfish sisters. This served to break the heart of her most tender sister, Jane, for she was firmly attached to Mr. Darcy's younger friend. While Jane held no animosity toward Mr. Bingley or his sisters for abandoning them the past November, Elizabeth knew whom to blame. Caroline Bingley was a viper. Her sister, Mrs. Louisa Hurst, was almost her exact copy. They were abhorrent. But so was Mr. Bingley for his spinelessness.

27

Colonel Fitzwilliam, whom she had walked with on occasion while in Kent, placed the financial situation of a lady above her accomplishments. His skewed view of a woman's value had disappointed her.

Even her own father had a propensity to shirk his duties towards his wife and daughters by not providing for their futures, either in the form of funds or discipline and training. Instead, he made the female occupants of his home an object of scorn by laughing at them and calling them silly. His secondary weakness was his devotion to his books above his family. Despite her love for him, she knew him to be selfish.

Tucking her knees tightly to her chest, she spun in the small enclosure until her back was against the same wall as Mr. Darcy's. The little amount of light appearing at their feet left him in deep shadow. She could make out none of his features, so she knew he could not see her clearly either.

Blatantly, she stuck her tongue out at him.

Oh, she had wanted to do that since the first night at the Meryton assembly when he had publicly declared her only tolerable, certainly not pretty enough to tempt him.

How his offense had earned her scorn. Until he burst through the doorway into their closet, she had figured on her resentment lasting a lifetime. Truly, he had been the most unpleasant man on the planet.

Next, she thumbed her nose at him. Aware she was covered in dirt from head to toe, she wiped off the streak of dust she must have left on her face with the back of her sleeve.

She giggled. *What else could she do?* Where the darkness was a torment to him, to her it was freedom to express her ire at a man who had believed himself superior to her and the inhabitants of Meryton.

"Would you share your humor?" he asked. "Because I see nothing which could possibly be a source of humor, Miss Elizabeth."

"Then, you would be wrong." Admittedly, it was easy in the blackness to be bold. "I will not lie to you, Mr. Darcy. Just now, I stuck my tongue out and thumbed my nose at you as well. You did not see, therefore, my actions were done with impunity."

She could hear him draw in a deep breath before he asked, "Are you satisfied with the results of your actions."

"I am," she admitted.

"Then, despite being your target, I am pleased for you." His reply was bland. "You are a woman of many more accomplishments than I had heard from Miss Bingley. If only she knew, she could add them to her list."

Elizabeth could not contain her mirth.

When he continued in mocking imitation of Bingley's sister with, "A woman must have a thorough knowledge of music, singing, drawing, dancing, and the modern languages, to deserve the word; and besides all this, she must possess a certain something in her air and manner of walking, the tone of her voice, her address and expressions, the length of her tongue when she chooses to display the appendage, the uplift to the end of her nose when gently manipulated by her shortest digit, or the word will be but half deserved,"

She burst into laughter.

Within a few short seconds, he joined in her joy.

"Gently manipulated?" she gasped. "I have never heard such hyperbole, sir."

"Now you know two things about me most, including longtime friends and family, do not know." He, too, quieted, his voice serious.

"Two? I count but one." She would not speak of his affliction.

"My morbid fear of being enclosed in a tight space?"

Surprised he mentioned it aloud, she nodded, forgetting he could not see her.

Seeking to catch him off guard, liking the fact he was out of balance, she said, "No, actually, I concluded your having a sense of humor as being what I learned about you."

He scoffed. "You are ignoring the elephant in the room by focusing on the ant."

"What does it matter? I have my own elephant with which to cope. I have no right, then, to tease you about yours."

"I say, I appreciate your fairness."

She heard his relief.

"I surprise you?" She peered at him, hoping to see him more clearly. Her efforts were in vain.

"Miss Elizabeth, my experience with females—both young and old, married or unattached—has been singular." He huffed. "By their actions and my observation, the man is expected to believe in the utter infallibility of the woman. She is always in the right, and he is always in the wrong. He serves to protect, while he is to be attached only to her while she flirts and teases to attract others. Fairness has little to with male/female relationships."

"Your opinion reeks of bitterness. This I am sorry to hear." Elizabeth was stunned at his openness. "We, as ladies, are taught to believe in the utter authority of the man."

"Ha! Would that be so."

She felt his movements as his elbow hit her side. She scooted away from him.

"My apologies." Gruffness laced each word. "I hate being cramped. My knees already ache from being drawn up to my chin."

"Then let us turn and face the far end of the closet. You can sit closest to our small glimpse of light," she suggested, wanting, for some reason, to ease his plight.

"Surely, you jest. Small glimpse of light?" he mocked. "...Do not forget the sheer magnitude of air drifting up from that massive gap," he quoted her earlier comment. "I will gratefully sit next to the 'massive gap' to protect you from the free flow of cold air sure to give an unprotected young lady a chill."

As he adjusted his position, she turned her back to him and moved to sit alongside him. It was a tight fit, her shoulder and arm pressed into his. However, the relief at having her legs stretched in front of her was grand. "I will admit that your quoting Miss Bingley word-for-word was a surprise. You remembering my comments under the stress of the moment is amazing."

Once settled, he asked, "The elephant you mentioned? Is it something you would be pleased to share?"

"I will freely do so should you reply to two concerns."

"I will."

"Have you always had a fear of the dark or was there an event that forever changed your view of small places?"

He sucked in a breath, and Elizabeth feared she had been too bold.

"No. I have not always feared being closed in."

"Sir, you do not have to share..."

"No, you not only asked, you aided me when I was unable to control my anxiety and you undoubtedly suffered because I could not. Should we ever be stuck inside a closet again with no way out, you should understand my difficulty."

"I cannot begin to imagine this happening more than once, but I will listen."

Clearing his throat, he began. With the almost painful recitation of the first words, Elizabeth knew he had been transported to a different place and time.

"As a youth, George Wickham, whom you know and admire as an officer in the militia stationed in Hertfordshire, was everything I could have wanted as a friend. When Richard would visit Pemberley, the three of us were inseparable." He chortled. "We called ourselves knights of the Round Table."

"You were Arthur?" She could see him wanting to be the hero king.

"Not at all, Miss Elizabeth. I was the youngest of the three, so George was King Arthur and Richard was the magician, Merlin."

"Something changed."

"Yes." He paused for the longest time.

Ready to suggest he not continue the tale, she was surprised when he began speaking.

"Before leaving for Eton, Wickham became aware of the differences in our station. His father was the steward of Pemberley. His mother, unrestrained in her spending, had placed the family in serious debt."

Elizabeth felt his arms move and speculated he was rubbing his face.

"He was not able to remain at school without my father's assistance. George was placed on an allowance. He hated being limited, and he came to hate me for being the heir to the largest estate he had ever seen. When the fellow students taunted him because of his reduced circumstances, he decided to change his future."

"Oh, no," Elizabeth whispered, knowing what was to come would not be good.

"Yes, oh no." Mr. Darcy drew up his legs. "George concluded, as only a fourteen-year-old could, that he would become the heir should something happen to me. I was twelve and still at home."

Stop! she silently pleaded. Mr. Wickham had been one of her favorites—a man without flaw. He was everything charming who told his stories of the harm done to him by the younger Mr. Darcy with a believability that cemented his reputation in Meryton as being unparalleled.

Darcy's baritone deepened as each word appeared forced from his mouth.

"One day, he suggested a game of hide and seek. Where I could never seem to escape Richard's pursuit, I had an easier time with George. This time was different. He blindfolded me and said he was leading me to a spot in Pemberley woods where I needed to find my way out, so I could search for him. I knew the woods like the back of my hand so stupidly and readily agreed. However, instead of a game, he had plotted to bury me alive in an abandoned mine shaft we had found years earlier."

His breathing quickened. "My arm broke in the fall. I was unaware because my head bashed against the rock wall on the way down. While I was unconscious, he shoveled in dirt until it seemed I was covered."

"Oh, Lord, no!" Elizabeth grabbed at his arm and pulled, hoping he would stop.

"I woke to darkness and intense pressure all around me, but mostly to my chest. I could not move. I could not breathe."

"How long?"

"How long was I there?" He removed his arm from her grip. "A day and a night." He huffed. "As an adult. I am aware I could not have been completely buried under the dirt and unable to take in air. As a child? I knew my death was imminent."

"I will never tease you or torment you for your fears, sir," Elizabeth readily admitted, her disgust at viewing Wickham as good company showed not only the flaw in her opinions, but her inability to discern character as well. "Why has he not been punished?"

"My father would not believe his godson capable of doing wrong."

Elizabeth was horrified at the lack of anger in Mr. Darcy's voice.

"George told him we were playing games, that I tripped and clumsily fell over my own growing feet, and there was a cave-in. My father believed him without question."

"Mr. Darcy!" She was affronted on his behalf. "How could your father not be aware of his perfidy?"

"My father was an intelligent man, gifted as a master who inspired love and devotion from all under his care. George Wickham's father was a good, moral man." He huffed. "To this day, I know not how they were blinded. It puzzles me exceedingly."

"Snakes," she blurted.

"Snakes?"

She wanted to chuckle at his confusion, yet with the conversation, it would have been highly inappropriate.

"My fear of snakes is as deep-seated and firm as your hatred of darkness. They frighten me when I see them unexpectedly to the point I cannot move. My heart races, my body shakes, and I break into sobs. If I see an illustration of one in a book, it slips from my fingers to the floor, never to be opened by me again. Should John Lucas or another neighborhood boy taunt me with one, I vow revenge in the worst manner possible as they know of my aversion." It was her turn to hesitate as serpents crawled across her mind's eye. "I do not like speaking of them or thinking of them because they tend to invade my dreams, turning them to nightmares. I wake the whole house screaming, so there is good reason my sisters never tease me because of my affliction."

"John Lucas has taunted you?"

"He did when we were much younger."

"I will seek revenge for you, Miss Elizabeth. Should I see him I will punch his nose, bloodying it and blackening his eye."

"You are too late, sir. I have already done such." She snickered wickedly. "He bore the evidence of my ire for weeks and has avoided me since."

"Can I ask how old you were?"

"I was nine-years-old. Even though he was slightly older, I towered over him. He has since outgrown me by a long distance. However, all I need to do is show him my fist, and he cowers. I feel empowered knowing I intimidate him."

"Despite being rather tiny?"

She heard his smile.

"My diminutive size is no barrier to fierceness. Pray remember that fact should you displease me more than you already have."

Laughter was sweet release. Time had passed, hard conversations were shared, and Elizabeth was starting to feel comfortable in their situation. It was her opinion that Mr. Darcy was comfortable as well.

"How long do you believe we will be here?" she had to ask.

"Long enough, Miss Elizabeth."

Although his words were cryptic, Elizabeth understood. A few moments spent alone would not breach the rules of propriety. Long minutes, possibly hours, would bind them together where the only way out would be either her ruin or their matrimony.

"We are in trouble, Mr. Darcy."

"Of that I am well-aware."

Four

DARCY

"I have never asked this of a woman before, but might I hold your hand in mine?" The wait until he felt the muscles in her upper arm flex seemed like hours. She had apparently wiped the surface of her palm down her skirt because he felt no grit when he was finally able to wrap her fingers in his. "We must speak of my aunt's expectations."

"I suppose we must." Elizabeth's reluctance surprised him. Until then, she had been bold in her speech. As a matter of note, so had he.

"I have never offered for Anne and will not, no matter how hard her mother pushes. Anne desires to live at Rosings until her life ends." He swallowed. "The doctor is treating her for a failing disease. She has never been strong. Anne longs for peace."

"She longs for the release death brings?"

"I…well, yes, she has told me she would rather sleep forever than live with the life quality she has now." Oh, God in heaven, he felt tears at the corners of his eyes. "My sadness for her, at times, overwhelms me. Richard, his siblings, my sister Georgiana, and I are all brimming with health and vigor. How can she not resent us for what we have always had and the potential for our futures?"

"I live with five other females, all with varying temperaments." Miss Elizabeth squeezed his fingers. "Women have a different outlook than men in this matter. We know going into a marriage of our chances of dying in childbirth. Does it keep us from wanting children? Not at all. From the time we reach our adolescent years, we know where that path can lead, despite how active or healthy we have been until then."

"You fear marriage?" He was unsettled at the thought.

"I do not," she quickly reassured him. "However, I will seriously consider the quality of man I marry, for he needs to be loved by me enough that I could both live for him and die for him as well."

He could not speak. *This is what she wants? How can this be?*

"What of ladies who care not if they love their husbands? How, with your reasoning, do they justify their decisions?" This made no sense.

"Think, Mr. Darcy. What is it they seek? For them, they calculate the cost of the potential for the loss of life to the gain they desire most, perhaps a title or wealth." She took in a deep breath and exhaled slowly. "This only applies when the lady has the freedom of choice. Oftentimes, a marriage is arranged with no thought to the lady's preferences. Imagine the heartbreak if a woman feels no love for her mate and has received little recompense. She may die as a sacrifice to the desire of her parents, not hers."

"Then she is more to be pitied." He thought of the marriages of his peers where the wife did die so the man would have an heir. What a loss to both should the babe be a girl child who might not inherit.

"It seems a waste, does it not?" she agreed.

"You will not do this, will you? Accept an arrangement without love and respect?" He needed to know.

"Before I was captured by the door to this passage and you found your way inside, I would have claimed, 'never'."

He appreciated her honesty. Darcy would rather not be blind to her concerns.

"We must marry or you and your sisters face ruin."

"I know," she whispered.

"I would not dishonor you by not offering my hand." He hoped she felt relief. He also hoped she would learn he was not the miscreant Wickham surely painted him to be.

Miss Elizabeth sighed.

"I am not the only one to suffer, sir. To be fair, by your coming to my rescue, your future has changed as much as mine. We are, neither of us, at fault."

"Thank you for your consideration. I do not deserve your kindness."

"Ha, kindness? How can this be?" She snorted. "You have no idea how I have bandied about your name in Hertfordshire, condemning you for creating hardship for Mr. Wickham and for arrogantly insulting me. I believe my most common words described your prideful arrogance and selfish disdain for the feelings of others."

He sucked in air as pain ripped through his chest. *This was her opinion of him?*

"I…I do not know how to respond," he honestly admitted.

"I cannot help but believe your aunt would have much to say on the subject," she offered.

"She has much to say on any subject." Turning his head towards where she sat, he asked, "You are not intimidated by Lady Catherine, are you?"

"Are you aware of a good reason why I should be?"

He shook his head, then remembered she could not see him. "No."

"I cannot find humor in your aunt. She is far too predictable."

He found humor in Miss Elizabeth.

"What of you, sir?" She leaned into his shoulder. "You act the devoted nephew in coming to her home each spring. Nonetheless, you do not allow her to control your decisions."

"I am my own man. I answer to no one."

"You seem excessively proud of your position, if I might say so." The slowness of her response clued him to the seriousness of her comment. Sudden awareness had him rethinking his reply.

"I was raised to take pride in being a Darcy. I was brought up with good principles, but not instructed in their application. My view of my own importance has been addressed by Richard. He feels it his purpose in life to humble me. Nonetheless, hearing the negative opinion from a lady I admire is far more successful than anything he has tried, I freely admit." He shrugged. "The poor man will have to live with his disappointment."

Miss Elizabeth patted the back of his left hand with the one he did not currently have in his grasp.

"You admire me?"

He was not at all surprised she noted the comment, which he had made purposefully.

"I do."

"Hmmm!" she mused. "I have found some…things, or I should clarify, some qualities to recently admire in you as well."

"Really? I am all amazement. Pray, do not keep me in suspense."

"Sir, I chose not to ask what you found admirable about me. Should I be first to confess my observations of you?"

He adored how she felt free to tease. Their banter (and the slim amount of light coming into the wardrobe) soothed him.

"No, sir, I will not allow you to tell me…yet. I will speak to your good features before I rejoice in hearing mine." Again, she leaned into his shoulder. "Besides your small flicker of a sense of humor, I have discovered you possess a measure of humility. Your strong affection for your family members, even irascible Lady Catherine, speaks of someone who knows the definition and value of sacrifice. While your devotion to Mr. Bingley and your care of him in Hertfordshire was admirable, you did not demand his acquiescence. Rather, it appeared you explained a task and allowed your friend to follow through on his own."

"Thank you, Miss Elizabeth." He courageously placed his free hand upon hers. "Your kind words are burned on my memory. I will cherish them forever."

"I am only grateful you did not follow the lead of Mr. Bingley's sisters, unlike their brother. I blame my Jane's heartbreak solely on the well-dressed shoulders of those two females."

"Your sister is heartbroken? She was in love with Bingley? I did not see it at all."

Pulling her hands away from any contact with his skin, she stated, "I cannot imagine why you would think otherwise, sir. She was fully devoted to him."

He heard her swallow.

She continued, "In truth, I had incorrectly assumed his heart was attached to my sister. Thus, I encouraged her to trust her feelings. What a fool I was— my own arrogance knew no bounds."

Darcy said nothing as his mind considered who actually was to blame. He knew it was not only Miss Bingley and Mrs. Hurst who convinced Bingley to abandon Hertfordshire. Darcy, out of fear for his growing attachment to the second Bennet daughter, strongly discouraged Bingley's pursuit of the eldest. A clean break appeared to be the best solution for them both.

Now, he regretted his involvement. An honorable man would confess his guilt. He was an honorable man.

"Miss Elizabeth, about Bingley and your sister…" Dread filled him at the hurt and anger that was to come. With his declaration, their good rapport would be gone. Already, before saying a word, Darcy regretted the loss.

Five

ELIZABETH

She was livid. All of the warm feelings Elizabeth had started to have for Mr. Darcy vanished in an instant.

Standing, she slapped her hands against the cupboard door after moving to the far end of the space. Moving her fingers with speed, she desperately searched for a means of escape.

"Get up and help," she demanded of Mr. Darcy. "You only assumed I searched thoroughly when you entered the room. I am but a silly female as my father often tells me. I could have overlooked a lever the size of your head. Then you would not have been trapped inside with me, and I would not now be obligated to an imbecile."

"I deserve your wrath."

She could tell by the movement of the air that he bowed.

"Yes, you do," she muttered, her hands continuing their exploration. "Where are we, do you know? Oh, wait! You know absolutely everything there is to know about everything, do you not?"

Tart words flowed off her tongue. How could he, a man she had been coming to respect, have forced apart two tender hearts? Those were the actions of a despicable man.

"I hate you!" she whispered to herself, trying out the words for sound. She had not said that phrase to any human since John Lucas and the snake. Their harshness pierced her inner ear. When no greater harm befell her from her abuse, she tried again, her voice slightly louder. "I loathe you. I despise you."

"I hear you," he sharply replied. He, too, stood to look for a button to release the door back into the passageway, the way from which they both had entered the closet.

For a long while, the only noise in the wardrobe was the sound of them moving in their selected space.

Her emotions had flared into an inferno as Mr. Darcy explained his reasoning for convincing Mr. Bingley to turn his back on the love of his life. Nevertheless, as her hands roamed over the trim around the wooden pieces, a tendril of memory, like the first hint of smoke from a fire, invaded her thinking.

Mr. Bingley had left. He had chosen to listen to his friend and sisters rather than remain devoted to Jane. It had been his decision to not stand firm.

While Jane would never find reason for blame in Mr. Bingley, his inconstancy bothered Elizabeth.

Could she respect a gentleman who was unable to withstand pressure from family? Not at all.

Her anger waned.

"You should not have involved yourself in a personal matter between them," she spoke aloud. "It was badly done, Mr. Darcy. Badly done."

He must have stopped searching, his hands possibly dropping to his sides as the only noise in the small space was generated from her.

"Do you see what I mean, Miss Elizabeth?" His tone overflowed with irritation.

Her anger flared.

"How can you be upset, sir? You, who are clearly in the wrong?" Her hands were on her hips as her upper body leaned towards him.

He growled. "Were we outside this confinement, I would depart your company immediately. *This* was what I referred to earlier when I told you females insisted upon their own infallibility. You see, now I am in possession of the facts, I freely admit I was wrong. Are you puffing up with pride at being right, Miss Elizabeth Bennet?" Each syllable snapped.

"How dare you!"

"I dare because no matter my words or actions, in your eyes, I will be wrong. I will be the unforgiven one. You, for the simple providence of being born a female, who badly misjudged Mr. Wickham are allowed to remain without blame for so doing. I, on the other hand, who also misjudged cannot be forgiven because I was born a son."

"You broke their hearts."

"You slandered my good name," was his quick rebuttal.

"You are unfair."

"Am I? Am I truly?"

He had moved closer—close enough she could feel his breath on her face. Despite the heat of anger, she had no fear of him. He would not harm her.

Spinning, she presented her back to him.

Jumbled, fragmented reflections of their earlier conversation and her own impressions warred inside her until she finally glimpsed clarity.

"I hate being wrong." Dropping her chin to her chest, she slowed the breath passing through her clenched teeth.

"And I do not?" he challenged.

Hugging her arms around herself, she huffed into the darkness.

"I hate that you are right," she confessed. "My sins against you are many. I now can only be ashamed for what I have done." It was hard to admit her flaws to him, of all men. "I, too, now have reservations about Mr. Bingley's suitability for the position of husband to my sweet Jane. She cannot see bad in anyone. While it is a boon for me as it means she loves me without reservation, it could create immense hardship if the man she relied upon was not firm in his decisions."

"I…you…we…" he cleared his throat. "We have argued, and reason has prevailed upon us both? Am I correct?"

"I hear your surprise, sir," she teased, her humor almost completely restored. "I much prefer to consider our canvassing the subject as a heated exchange of ideas. Argue sounds rather common, do you not think?"

She had caught him off guard. She had no need to see his face to know he was pondering whether or not to smile.

"We survived."

Elizabeth heard the wonder in his tone. Chuckling, she added, "We have endured to…to debate another day, I suspect."

"Have you found anything?" He wisely changed the subject.

"I have found nothing more than what I found earlier." Dejected, she stepped back to the wall and sat down. "Feel free to search where I have done. My prejudices have been exposed, so the humiliation of having you see something I did not will, I suppose, vanish as soon as the doors open."

Surprisingly, he chose to be seated as well. She had assumed he would have gone back over her search area with the confidence of discovering a latch to release the door she had failed to see.

"Miss Elizabeth, I have no reason not to trust that your exploration was thorough. Neither of us has succeeded in finding a means of escape. Yet, both of us had our sins laid out for exposure. While I wish you had not shared your disapprobation of me with others, had I acted the gentleman in the first place, you would have had nothing to say."

Considering his comment thoroughly, she harrumphed. "Then we have discerned we are two imperfect people."

"Yes, this is true. With that said, are not all people flawed? Even your Jane. Can you say she is absolutely perfect?"

Elizabeth giggled. "No, for by day she is kindness personified, but at night her snores keep me awake for hours. My goal each evening is to fall deeply asleep before she does."

Slapping her hand over her mouth, she shook her head at herself. "I should not have said a word. Have I learned nothing?" Elizabeth muttered into her fingers.

"Miss Bennet's secret is safe with me." Mr. Darcy paused. "Once we are released, I will write to Bingley with a full explanation and apology for intervening in his affairs. You may read the missive should it relieve your mind. I will make certain it contains no mention of her nocturnal noise."

She snorted.

"I do not find it necessary to see your letter in advance, sir," she admitted. "Mr. Darcy, I am hesitant to mention our 'debate' but I find it a bit of a miracle how we were able to address volatile topics with barely any harm to ourselves. Do you not find this extraordinary?"

He chuckled. "In truth, I find you extraordinary, Miss Elizabeth. Since the day you arrived at Netherfield Park to care for your sister during her illness, you have challenged me in more ways than any other female has done, including my sister."

"Tell me of your sister. Is she much younger than you?" Her question was innocently asked. Nonetheless, his quizzical response put her on guard.

"How do you know she is younger than me? Who has spoken of her?" Before she could respond, he tapped the back of his head against the wall as his chin must have risen. "Oh, Richard must have told you of Georgiana. He shares guardianship so knows her character well."

"No, your cousin was not my source," she hesitatingly mentioned. "I heard of her from Mr. Wickham."

"Again, he rears his ugly head," Darcy muttered.

She felt the instant tightening of his arms and inherently knew his hands were fisted.

"I now wonder at how believable his tale was, sir," Elizabeth offered. "His mention of her was slight in comparison to his condemnation of you. Therefore, might I hear from your own mouth the truth of her?"

"He treated her harshly, in a way that both decried his claims of being a gentleman and destroyed her growing confidence in herself. His actions were treacherous as he sought to taint something beautiful and revenge himself against me." He gasped.

"Mr. Darcy?" Concerned, she reached for his arm, and gave it a not-so-gentle shake.

"I closed my eyes. I could not see the light."

His breathing, at first rapid, was slowing.

"Then focus your gaze on that monstrous gap, sir." Imitating Lady Catherine, she used her elbow to jab him in the side. "Nephew, I command you to do as I say. Only if you obey my edicts to the smallest degree will you succeed in establishing yourself as a person of elevated rank."

He guffawed.

When he quieted, he easily admitted, "I do not understand you at all. You are half parts teasing and the other half tormenting. You are as unlike the ladies of the *ton* as could be. I do not know whether to toss you aside or hold onto you with a firm grip. I have never in my lifetime exposed my deepest fears and flaws to another human being. You cannot know how grateful I was when you responded with patience and tact. On one level, I trust you as I have never trusted another. When I finally relax in the comfort of your gentlest nature, you surprise me with a tease."

"Ah, sir, then I have become an exemplary accomplished woman for our charge, our internal makeup since the womb, is to unsettle an unattached man until he notices none other." Giggling, Elizabeth pinched the back of his arm, knowing she did no harm with the thickness of his coat fabric. "Yet, in this I fear I have revealed my constancy. Have you not comprehended my nature? Have you not sketched my character as one who would rather think of the past and the future with pleasure? I, for a certainty, am a realist, Mr. Darcy. I do not overlook or ignore life's harsh realities. They affect all of us, do they not?"

She felt the movement of his nod of agreement.

"Nevertheless, rather than allowing them to rob me of my pleasure in being alive, I do what I must to protect myself and those I love. Then I leave what I have no power or authority over to others more qualified."

"Hmmm…while your attitude is enlightening, it is I who often holds the power and authority. Until now, I had thought myself to be a good brother and master. You are forcing me to swallow my failings, in particular, my lack of humility." He mused, "I am not certain this is well-pleasing to me."

"I suppose not."

Relaxing back against the wall, an unexpected warmth and pressure filled Elizabeth from her waist to her hips.

Oh, Good Lord! All the tea she had sipped to have something with which to occupy the long minutes in Lady Catherine's drawing room was making its liquid presence known. Elizabeth wanted to bash her head on the thick wood behind her. Embarrassment and sudden misery consumed her.

"Pardon me, Mr. Darcy," she turned her face away from him, despite knowing he could not see her in the darkness. "I believe now is one of those opportunities you will have to test your wisdom and authority in arranging matters for both of our comfort for I have not a clue what to do."

"Yes, Miss Elizabeth? How might I be of assistance?"

Did he have to sound so…so…so patronizing? Well, what she had to ask would bring him solidly back to earth.

"I believe we have a problem which can only be alleviated by escape and a quick visit to a private location to refresh myself." Elizabeth blurted it out when the weight of the contained fluid became painful, uncaring if he thought less of her for speaking of something *never* discussed with someone of the male sex. In fact, it was the role of genteel females to pretend bodily functions did not exist.

"Oh," discernment had to have hit him like a brick randomly dropped from above. "I…pray forgive my blunt speech but men do not have difficulty admitting the need to relieve…ah, I understand."

Jumping up from where he sat, he felt his way along the wall until he reached the far corner. From the sounds, Elizabeth knew he stomped his boot heel into the floor close to the outer door.

He must have jumped as she heard his head hit the ceiling before both feet crashed down on the bottom of the closet. The vibration from the blow shook the cupboard, but apparently, nothing moved. "Blast it! I am sorry, Miss Elizabeth. My attempts were unsuccessful." As he stepped forward, his tone softened. "As an alternate option, I would ask that you lift your skirt and…"

"What?" *How could he?*

Rising quickly, she challenged him with her fist.

Except, he could not see. When he immediately spoke again, she heard his resignation, "as I was saying, lift your skirt and remove your petticoat. The softness and fullness of the fabric can be bunched together so it…well, the cloth will absorb…I will place it as far away as possible, I…ah, I find I share your situation. I, too, drank too much tea."

"Oh, well…"

Doing as he suggested, the momentary relief was worth her chagrin. When they passed each other to exchange places, pressing her chest to his in the tight confines, she closed her eyes tightly and covered her ears. *Could the situation possibly get worse?*

Six

DARCY

As time passed, the heat in Darcy's face and neck receded. He was certain her discomfort matched his. Yet, she had not uttered one word of repudiation to his suggestion, nor had she complained at the odd solution to their problem. He was eternally grateful the floor had warped to be lower at the end where the soiled garment rested, or they could not be sitting where they were.

Once their needs had been seen to and they once again had their sides pressed firmly together as they sat on the floor, the dust they had stirred started to settle. He sneezed repeatedly. Then, she did.

He glanced at the light peeking from under the door. Slipping his fingers under the wood, he discovered the exit to be extremely thick, a relic from his uncle's youth when furniture was heavy enough to need several strong men to relocate it should it be desired.

Approximately six inches from where his back touched the wall, his hand encountered the heavy leg of whatever obstruction held the doors closed. Apparently, the weight was on the top as the post was not excessively wide. Possibly a massive bed with a heavy headboard where the diminutive former master of Rosings Park once rested.

Having calculated their position by mentally retracing their path, he was fairly certain they were in the family portion of the west wing, in particular, the former room of his deceased uncle.

Searching his memory, he recalled the few times he had been inside the chamber. It was when Lewis de Bourgh was in the sick bed for the final time. Closing his eyes tightly, Darcy struggled to remember. Odd. The wardrobe had been situated against the northern wall in an alcove facing east so anyone entering the room would have only seen the side of the piece rather than the front. The bed, on the other hand, had been flanked by large windows on the western wall. As with all suites, there was an adjoining dressing room where the majority of the master's clothing would be kept.

Hmmm. Clarity struck.

"Elizabeth," In his excitement he failed to note his informality. "After climbing the two staircases, how many turns did we make?"

"Just one at the end of the second set of stairs."

He agreed. "I believe I know why moving the wardrobe doors has been impossible."

He could see in his mind's eye her brow lifting and wanted to smile at the image.

He continued, "The turn placed us so we entered the wardrobe as it faced the opposite wall of an alcove. I believe someone pushed the bed and possibly other furniture into this same alcove, filling it completely, so any efforts to budge the door would be futile."

"Oh, no. This is not good news."

He was unsurprised her sharp mind had understood their dilemma.

"I believe we have been attempting to break down the wrong door."

As one, they spun their positions and squeezed together as tightly as possible, so their legs could hit their entry portal at the same time.

"It is a good thing I regularly enjoy a long walk, is it not?" she chuckled.

Oh, Lord. His mind went blank as a picture of firmly muscled legs on the shape of a pretty woman crossed his mind, staying planted directly behind his eyes. Vivid recollections of renaissance paintings he had seen in various museums where women's forms were soft, and round were an antithesis to what he thought her figure would be. She was narrow at the shoulders and hips but rounded where…

He cleared his throat.

"Shall we begin, Mr. Darcy?" she sweetly inquired.

He wanted to slap himself for the inappropriate, disrespectful brain encased in his thick skull. If she ever knew his thoughts, he expected she would not hesitate to slap him instead.

"Yes, Miss Elizabeth. Let us begin."

They kicked against the door with all their might. The sound was deafening—to them.

Once stopped, they were again covered in dust and dirt. Despite their coughing from the churned up dust, the door, which had a different sound than the one behind them at the blows, had a large crack at the bottom. Hope blended with jubilation.

Grabbing her hand, he squeezed. At this unspoken signal, they began again. In moments, the panel gaped enough Miss Elizabeth could squeeze through. Repeated pounding made the hole large enough for him.

Happiness and the joy of accomplishing a heroic feat moved him to do the unthinkable. Releasing her hand, his arms, on their own, wrapped around her shoulders and pulled her to his chest. She fit perfectly as he had long suspected would be the case.

Horrified at his own temerity, he let go at once. Fitzwilliam Darcy was a proper man. Always. He had never embraced a woman other than his sister when she was much younger. And, his mother, of course.

"I…Miss Elizabeth…pray forgive the impulse of the moment." As bad as he had blushed at having to relieve himself on Miss Elizabeth's petticoat, which they would gratefully leave behind once they exited the closet, the heat covering his cheeks from this last act was worse than the first.

"Do not concern yourself, sir. No one witnessed your reaction, and I felt the same need for celebration."

Her voice was level. He could hear no remonstration. His own guilt would suffice, he suspected, to punish him for the breach in propriety.

He was ridiculous. Should no one find them in the next few hours (for he had no worries his cousin would not meet with success once he returned to Rosings), the impact to Miss Elizabeth's reputation was already complete. They were well and truly compromised. She would, if he could convince her to the necessity, become his wife.

He smiled to himself. Relief, greater than that at the idea of their impending escape, flooded him. Only his need to facilitate their release aided his mind to refocus. Running his hands around the jagged edges of the opening, he considered the best angle for exiting.

Beyond the hole was sheer darkness.

When he did not immediately use their escape, she asked, "Are you well, sir?"

He had no clue how to respond, his emotions were conflicted until he could no longer understand himself.

"Mr. Darcy," she hesitantly caught his attention before he could offer an answer. "When might we expect…do you think someone is coming to our aid?"

He sighed heavily, looking back at her, glimpsing the narrow shaft of light.

"Unfortunately, with Richard gone, oversight of our search party is in the hands of my aunt, with the assistance of Mr. Collins." The news was not good. "I have been hoping Lady Catherine's butler, Smyth, will give instructions to the staff to systematically cover Rosings from top to bottom. I have yet to hear anyone attempt to enter the room containing the closet."

"Might the door be locked?"

"The housekeeper should have a master key to unlock all of the doors on her chatelaine." He again ran his hands over the hole, hoping he would be able to pass through it with some of his dignity intact. "I cannot imagine a reasonable person not realizing a passage from the library would go to the master's chambers. Mine does at Pemberley." He desperately wanted to comfort her, to provide assurance of a quick rescue. However, unless Smyth followed his own natural inclinations, who knew where Lady Catherine would send the maids and footmen?

"Somehow, reasonable is not a word I connect with my father's cousin."

"I would say the same of my aunt."

Elizabeth gave an unladylike snort. "Then again, Mr. Collins did choose to offer for Charlotte, who is known for her practical wisdom."

"Yet, she chose him, did she not?" he quipped, enjoying their brief respite.

"She did." Miss Elizabeth sighed. "I fear necessity made her decision rather than affection, much like…"

"Us?" he speculated where her mind traveled.

Darcy desperately wanted to tell her how his feelings had gone from rejection in Hertfordshire to desire in Kent. He yearned for her to know the inclination of his heart and return his tender emotions.

Despite the heat of their "debates" since being enclosed together, he looked forward to future lively exchanges of thoughts and opinions. Her active brain had no difficulty keeping up with his more educated mind. In actuality, he was shockingly pleased to admit to her being his mental superior.

"Yes, like us," Miss Elizabeth sighed.

He did not like hearing her despair at the idea of being permanently tied to him. For him to be happy, he needed to guarantee her happiness. Should she deny him this task, they would both suffer in misery. But, maybe his thinking was wrong. Perhaps her despair came from being forced to marry rather than freely accepting his offer. Suddenly, he felt better.

Deciding to attend to that idea later, he noted, "Miss Elizabeth, we may have many hours yet until we step outside the passage." When she started to speak, he raised his hand, forgetting she could not see him. He plunged ahead. "I have every confidence in Richard's ability to hunt us down and then torment us with our current circumstances. With that said, I will listen to him boast until my hair has turned grey and we both stoop when we stand if he will be the means of release from this trap we are in."

"Mr. Darcy, I cannot know how much time has passed since we left the drawing room for the library. The days are longer than in winter, but the setting sun will place the room outside the closet in darkness. There will be no light. Once we step back into the passage and turn the corner, there will only be blackness. I am worried for you when our slim source of air and relief is gone. I ask again, how you are faring?"

Oh, God in heaven! He closed his eyes, which was foolish in the situation. Would she yet see him curled tightly into a ball as he cowered and shook from fright? How could he survive should Richard not find him, either from the mortification of having her witness his weakness or from his heart bursting at the panic?

He could not breath. There was no air. Slapping out at the door, he climbed over her legs to sit back against the closet exit, so his feet could again pound at the wood still remaining around the hole. His need to yell for help, screaming at the top of his lungs was viable enough he almost followed through.

Pressing the bottom of his hands into his eyes, he sought calm.

Warmth. Pressure against his shoulder and a light weight across his back. Though his mind was aware of her presence, of her squeezing her slim fingers around the muscles in his left arm, it was the fragrance of her drifting into his nostrils that finally caught his attention.

"Sir," she whispered directly into his ear. "Feel the air bubbling up from the massive gap. See the light coming in? You can breathe and so can I because the volume of air is immense. Open your eyes, Mr. Darcy, and look at me. See that I am alive and healthy. Feel my breath on your cheek? I do this because there is oxygen in abundance. Pray, sir, breathe in. Then breath out."

He heard her. He obeyed.

Once the pounding of his heart receded, he dropped his head back to the wooden surface behind him. His mortification from his panic was complete. Surely, she had not a fragment of respect left for him, if she had had any in the first place.

"Mr. Darcy, I hear someone." Excitedly, she dropped her arms from around him and turned back to the wardrobe door.

How could he be thrilled at the idea of release and saddened at the same time for no longer being in her embrace? He was a fool.

Seven

ELIZABETH

"What was…?"

"Did you…?"

They both quieted to see if the noise repeated itself, holding their breath while they waited. When metal scraped metal and the sound of an unused door being open reached their ears, they turned to face the closet door to yell for help.

Before Elizabeth could open her mouth, Lady Catherine barked out, "Why are you breaking into Sir Lewis' room? There is no one there. That girl has abandoned us to follow her wild ways, and Darcy has certainly gone after Fitzwilliam. Return to your duties immediately."

At that, the door slammed shut and the lock was reengaged.

Elizabeth slapped the closet door with her palm so hard the sting brought tears to her eyes. When she started to yell, Mr. Darcy stopped her.

"Elizabeth, do not." He captured her hand in his, holding it firmly.

"What? Why? What are you about, Mr. Darcy? We could have been rescued. Have you lost your mind?" She was furious, and her ire was fully towards him. Her dress was stiff from the dirt and grime, her hands were filthy, she mostly likely had cobwebs in her hair, and her petticoat was soaked and smelling in the corner. It was not her best day.

He huffed. "Not at all. Pray listen to reason."

"Your explanation for stopping me had better be good, sir, or I will change my inclination and hold a grudge against you for the rest of my days."

He sighed, then sat back against the wall.

"Think, Miss Elizabeth, of the consequences should we be found here by my aunt, of all people. She would be blind to our true circumstances. All she would see is our having spent a length of time in her husband's bed chambers—alone."

"You are saying you would like to hand-select our rescuer?" She could not force the sarcasm away. It built in her and erupted as soon as she opened her mouth.

"No, however, should Smyth or Richard find us, we would not be immediately exposed to a cross-examination where the questioner already assumed knowledge of the facts. We could have our needs tended to with little fuss."

"Mr. Darcy," she began, only to be interrupted.

"Yes, I am Mr. Darcy. You are Miss Elizabeth. Nonetheless, we are compromised, we are cramped together in a closet, we have…" he cleared his throat, "shared the same…uh, the same petticoat for the same purpose, and we will leave this wardrobe engaged to marry should you be wise enough to accept my hand. I cannot imagine any more intimate circumstances an unattached couple could be in other than actually sharing the marriage bed which we will not do until we wed. Therefore, would you agree we could address each other less formally?"

"Should I be *wise enough*?" Seething, she balled up her fist to strike, mentally convincing herself it would be in her best interest.

"Out of everything I said, *that* is all you heard?"

She heard his anger. In her opinion, he had no right to it.

"Firstly, you have already called me Elizabeth more than once. Secondly, I cannot call you by your first name because I think of Colonel Fitzwilliam when I hear it. And, lastly, but most importantly, I cannot believe you to be entirely without sense although it appears to have abandoned you completely." Elizabeth enunciated each syllable. "You simply cannot assume I will be your wife when you have yet to offer for me. Either you are getting ahead of our situation or you dreamed you proposed marriage and I accepted. I have not." She was definite. "However, the reality is I will not accept a man who would not find pleasure in pleasing me. I would not accept a man I did not want to please. I would not accept a man who believes he knows what is best for me without asking my opinion. I would not."

She would give anything, a kingdom if she had one, to leave this room and this man. He infuriated her like no other. With no other outlet for her frustration, she kicked the bottom of the paneling at his side. Except, she missed.

"Oof!" he moaned.

Regret at assaulting him warred with pleasure that she had put her full weight behind the blow. *She was a bad lady, definitely not how her mother trained her to be*. He would bear the bruise mark for a long time, she feared.

"I apologize."

"You are not sorry at all. I hear the perverse thrill in your tone, Elizabeth Bennet." He stood. "Well, this settles the matter."

"How?" She wondered at him. Certainly, her personality was long established in going from anger to laughter or the other way around. His? He puzzled her exceedingly. A full range of emotions had been displayed by him during their captivity. *Who was this man?* Could she marry him? Would she marry him? Him?

He leaned back against the wood, then sighed heavily, as if the world's weight bore him down. "Elizabeth, you ask questions and make statements tough for a man to answer. We of the male sex are not taught by our fathers nor our masters to address these topics. In my years at University, we were offered no classes on comprehending the mind of a woman. Thus, I mean no disrespect if I do not respond quickly. Pray allow me time to honestly consider how best to react and reply." He chuckled to himself. "Also, know I accept your kick as a warning to better guard my tongue and my thoughts."

"Then I will make this easier." Her ire was beginning to abate. "In your opinion, am I a woman worthy of being pleased?"

"Absolutely." His response was without hesitation.

"Since I cannot call you Fitzwilliam, how should I address you?"

"My Lord? Master? Grand Instructor?" he teased.

Her elbow flew out and jabbed him in the same side her foot had targeted.

"Ouch!"

"Be warned," she sneered. "I am not without resources."

"Ha! You are the most dangerous type of female on the planet." He paused. "But, despite my apparent lack of good sense, I find myself wanting to attach you to me for my lifetime. Are you worthy of being pleased? I find I could easily spend each minute of the day doing so. And, you may call me William."

He had left her completely unsettled. In truth, he excited her. Their verbal volleys delighted her each time he returned as he had received. His mind was quick. His emotions were raw. Elizabeth felt equal parts anger and compassion, feeling his pain in her own heart.

Could she spend a lifetime with him? The question was moot. They were compromised. Unless she accepted an offer he had yet to make, her ruin would be complete and shared with her innocent sisters.

"William," she whispered, trying out the name to see how it fell from her lips.

"Did your mother not train you to be acquiescent?" he taunted.

"Did your father not train you to be a gentleman?" was her quick rebuttal.

"Will you marry me?" He slipped the question into their exchange as if it had no more importance than asking if she liked her bread with butter.

Deciding to reply in kind, she blandly stated, "I might as well. I have had no better offers today and most likely will not with our isolation. Unless your wit can be agitated to consider an alternative, I suppose I will accept your offer."

"You will be my wife?" he quizzed, probably for clarity.

His torment during the past hour—or however long they had been in the wardrobe—had been complete. She could no longer tease.

"I will be your wife, William. I will wear your ring and wed you when it is arranged. I will show up at the chapel and say the expected vows while at the same time mentally omitting the promise to obey while, in reality, I promise to shake the ground you are walking upon for the next seventy years."

"You will, will you?" Darcy became completely serious. "I will do my best to be a good husband for you, Elizabeth. I will accord you the honor you deserve as mistress of our homes. I will be forever loyal. When I promise to cherish you during the recitation of the vows, my words will be sincere."

Her heart melted just a bit.

He added, "The other reason for waiting for my cousin to rescue us is our appearances. I find it difficult to think you would be pleased for a strongly opinioned woman to see you at less than your best. Richard, I promise, will not notice whether your gown is black or orange, whether your coiffure is secure or riddled with dust mites, or if you have dirt on your cheeks." Darcy insisted, "He will look at our countenance and then our eyes to determine our health and safety. I know my cousin. His concern will override his initial curiosity."

Elizabeth again, for the millionth time it seemed, reviewed their situation. He was right. She would not be presentable for public exposure.

"Then we should wait?" The thought was not entirely unpleasant. Mr. Darcy, no, William, had surprised her with his conversational abilities. "What should we discuss to pass the time?"

"Books?" he suggested.

She was pleased. Within seconds they were sharing opinions and questioning the preferences of each other. He was well-read. She appreciated his thoughtfulness and insight. The time flew by.

However, discomfort from sitting and leaning on hard surfaces was not their only hardship. When they completed a thorough review of their favorite Shakespeare comedy (*As You Like It*), Elizabeth was running her tongue over her lips at the end of every sentence. The moisture was needed to keep them from sticking together. The inside of her mouth was dry and her throat had a noticeable scratchy feeling at the back.

William must have been having the same difficulty. After clearing his throat and coughing, she felt his arm lift, his hand going to his face.

Doing the same, she wiped the layer of dust from around her mouth. It provided no relief.

"Elizabeth," he whispered, leaning towards her. "Are you thirsty?"

"Parched," she admitted. What she would give for a cool glass of water. She would even take a lukewarm thimbleful, swishing it around her mouth to ease the arid taste of nothing before gratefully swallowing the liquid.

"Since we are not sure when Richard will return, we need to preserve whatever moisture accumulates inside our mouth. I suggest we refrain from speaking as long as possible."

His suggestion was sound, making it an easy task to obey.

"Breathe through your nose, William. It will, I think, help. As well, try not to move so dust is stirred. Please?"

Closing her eyes, her mind shot to a rapidly changing picture book of water sources. Rivers, streams, ponds, oceans, and the elusive tall drink of water haunted her.

They could go for a long period of time without food. Without water? She knew from Jane's illness, where her high fever kept her from keeping fluids in her body, the pains induced by fluid depletion were extensive. Jane's thinking was not clear, she was weak and shaky, her head throbbed, and all she wanted to do was sleep.

Would this happen to them? Elizabeth shuddered.

"Are we going to die?" Her mind had automatically reached for and found the extreme to their situation. Once it had entered her thinking, she could not budge it from being all she could consider.

This time, it was William who reached to put his arm around her. Pulling her to him, her shoulder tucked in under his, his barely-there whiskers present on his cheek scratching her forehead.

She wanted to cry, but the trails of liquid pouring down her cheeks to the corner of her mouth would bring a salty taste to an already dry mouth. The loss of moisture would be insensible.

"I do not know," he finally answered. "I would give everything I own for it not to happen, but I simply do not know."

Eight

DARCY

It was uncomfortable to swallow. Darcy could not imagine what Elizabeth was going through. For some reason, the idea that his much larger size meant he had more internal moisture made him conclude she was suffering much more than he was. Reasoning was no longer important. Either way, they were in terrible trouble.

He was a fool. He should have called out to his aunt and dealt with the consequences of being exposed after their rescue.

Wracking his brain, he came up with absolutely nothing to ease their plight. Everything about them reeked of dryness.

Elizabeth. She was a marvel to him. As one who prided himself on being steadfast, her rapid change from anger to joy often bewildered him. Were her emotions shallow or did she feel the depth of them? He had to ask.

Her reply satisfied him … and saddened him.

"My mother holds onto resentment in a way that feeds her self-esteem. In so doing, it elevates her, at least in her own mind, as being superior to her foe, or in her case, foes."

"Plural?"

"Yes, many."

Her body crumpled with her sigh. He felt the weight of her change of position as she rested heavier against his shoulder.

"Unfortunately, my next youngest sister, Mary, is much the same. By searching out the flaws in others and continuing to build a case against any wrong done, her thinking is clouded from the self-righteousness simmering in her heart. She is an avid preacher against these offenses, where I believe being a godly teacher would help her learn principles of forgiveness. Should she, instead, let go of her acrimony, she would be much happier, I believe."

"You have learned from their experience, then?"

"I only wish it was that easy, William," Elizabeth scoffed. "I will tell you a secret I have not shared with Jane or my father. One, which when known, might leave you convinced of my treacherous heart."

"I cannot imagine." Darcy's curiosity was piqued.

"Then be prepared to be shocked in addition to being bewildered, for I only act as if I am no longer angry when the truth is, I am struggling with the hurt and pain I am carrying on the inside. I keep it locked away until I am alone to confront the demons released when my emotions are finally set free."

He heard her feet slide up to her chest and felt her lean forward to rest her forehead against her knees.

"I am a fraud, Mr. Darcy. You are getting the worst sort of woman for a bride, a female who only pretends to be happy when inside she is full of turmoil and strife. My family believes I remain unaffected by malicious actions or words."

He felt her hurt deeply. He was crushed. "This is why you laughed when you heard my insult at the Meryton assembly? You actually did not find the situation amusing?"

"Why would I? What female, or human being, would enjoy hearing they were only tolerable? You were the highest ranking unattached man of fortune to visit our area of Hertfordshire in my lifetime. Your comments wounded me, William. To retaliate, I did as my mother does and stirred up gossip against you. What a bitter shrew I am."

Lord! The offense was his alone.

"No, Elizabeth, do not say thus." He swallowed the little bit of moisture he had been able to gather. "The fault rests solely upon me."

"I knew you would claim this. I knew you would." Elizabeth dropped her legs down and leaned back. "There has been much revealed about your character while we have been confined. You gather accountability to yourself and hold onto it tightly, even that which does not belong to you. I will tell you as I do Mary: let it go."

"As you do?" he quickly responded.

"Ah, you see, it is much easier to be the instructor than the student. I endeavor to practice what I preach but fail regularly. Nevertheless, I am convinced letting go of resentment is the course of wisdom." Her head thumped as she rested it back against the wood. "For the most part, I *am* able to find humor in bad situations and, once I have taken out the pain and chewed on it for a long while, I can see the possible motives behind the unkind deed or words. Perhaps he or she was having a miserable day. Or, they misunderstood the circumstances and reacted poorly. Perhaps the initial wrong was mine and they reacted from hurt I unwittingly caused. I do not know."

Darcy recalled their first meeting.

"My rudeness was inexcusable," he insisted.

She snickered. "Yes, but it was understandable. I have not forgotten how you earlier described the approach most females have used to capture your attention. I, too, heard the whispers of your wealth as soon as you entered the room. You could not have known at the time that, unlike the others, I had no intentions towards you."

"Do you feel like laughing now?" he asked, running his tongue around the inside of his mouth to dampen the surfaces. Parched, the word she had earlier chosen, was fitting.

"I could if I felt the inclination. However, my concern for our situation outweighs my need to perform."

She must have smiled, though he assumed it would be deprecating.

"I would hope you no longer hide your true emotions from me, Elizabeth." The air burst from his lungs. His offer was bold for him. "I, too, will take off the mask I wear in public, so we can meet and come to know each other's true character."

"Your mask? The one with no smile?" she teased.

"Yes, that one." He grinned. Despite being in miserable circumstances, he was remarkably happy.

"William, I realize my mentioning my thirst is futile, but I think silence would be better served than conversation. My tongue wants to stick to the roof of my mouth."

"As does mine," Darcy admitted.

"Then I shall rest here thinking pleasant thoughts and hope you do as well," she suggested, moving back to lean upon him.

"I shall think of you." And, he did.

***

Time passed without them knowing whether it crawled as a turtle or raced like a rabbit. There was no way of knowing. Elizabeth had fallen into a restless sleep. He rejoiced at her soft purrs, quite unlike Jane Bennet's alleged snores.

When Elizabeth's head had first drooped toward his shoulder, he reached behind her and pulled her into him. With her firmly planted against him, he felt…complete.

Regulating his breathing, hoping the pounding in his head would match the slower pace, he worried about their survival. Would Richard think to look in this room? Surely, he would recall the matching passage at Pemberley. Or, perhaps not.

Searching the deepest recesses of his memory, Darcy could not recall showing his cousin the means of going from one room to the other at Pemberley. His father had not revealed the hidden latch to his son until Darcy reached his majority. By then, Richard was firmly ensconced in the military so rarely visited Derbyshire.

Frustrated, Darcy rubbed his face with his free hand. Then, for reassurance, he ran his hand under the door to feel the freedom beyond. They were so close.

The stale air of the passage crept into the cupboard, bringing the toxic mildew smell into their enclosure. Dipping his nose close to the top of her hair, Darcy inhaled a light scent of a flower reminding him of spring. And dust.

Sneezing to rid himself of the offending particles, he woke Elizabeth.

"I apologize. Pray pardon the noise," Darcy immediately insisted.

"No need." Lifting her head, she moved the hand resting against his chest. Pushing against him, she, to his regret, moved away from him. "I…"

Easing her embarrassment at waking to his tight embrace, Darcy sought to distract her with the conclusions he had reached during her nap.

"Elizabeth, although it is not my preference, I think we should move to the library end of the passage. If it were me, it would be the first room I would investigate. If we hear Richard enter, we could raise enough noise to penetrate the thick bookshelf comprising the passageway."

Once the decision was presented, he wanted to mock himself for his own stupidity.

"Good Lord, had we gone there from the start, we most likely would have been found for I believe the library would have been the room most searched by my aunt's staff." Disheartened, he wanted to sink into the floor. How would she ever learn to rely on him as husband and master of their estates if he missed something blatantly obvious that could have kept her from suffering? Argh!

"Mr. Darcy, William, we cannot go back in time. There is no sense attempting to swim in the mire of regret. Let us, instead, consider our options," Elizabeth calmly responded. "First and foremost, we need to remember there are two of us here, not myself alone. Where you needed the light and air from under the door, I needed companionship to keep me from going stark raving mad in the silence. Had we not found the wardrobe, we would have sat on cold, damp stone rather than a dry floor."

Her comment had barely left her mouth when they heard a loud pounding from the direction of the library. The sound quickly traveled through the dark hallway, up the stairs, and into their room. Richard was yelling their names.

"Here!" Darcy yelled back. "We are coming."

Scrambling to their feet, Darcy stepped through the hole in the door into the darkness. Reaching back to assist Elizabeth, he caught his final glimpse of the light. The now familiar fragments of panic started squeezing his chest.

"William," she pulled on his hand to free herself, then cupped his face to draw it down to hers.

His resistance was momentary.

Blowing softly into his face, she whispered, "Feel the air, William. There is more than enough to sustain us both as we hurry down the stairs. The darkness is no longer our enemy. Our greatest danger is navigating down the staircases safely to reach your cousin and freedom. Pray, feel the air," she again blew on his cheek.

He kissed her forehead, relieved to have her alongside him. Bravely, he clasped her hands in his own. He could do this. "Follow me."

Knowing there would be no stairs until they turned the corner, he easily moved them from the wardrobe to the far wall. At the bend, he dropped her hands to feel the wall. Again, he yelled for his cousin at the top of his lungs.

"Hold the tail of my coat, Elizabeth. Thus, you will feel each time I step down. Should I fall, let go." Despite feeling like the walls were pressing in upon him, he moved his foot forward. Finding nothing under the sole of his boot, he took the first stair moving them downward. The pull on his garment let him know she was with him. He took another step, shouting Richard's name at the same time.

"Do not let go," he needlessly reminded her. *Was he directing her or reassuring himself?* It mattered not.

"I will not, William. I will not let go."

On the eighth tread, when he slid his foot forward, he found solid ground.

The pounding in his heart matched the sounds coming from the library wall. Four steps forward, they reached the second set of stairs.

"Elizabeth." It was a struggle to breathe. "Speak to me. I need your voice."

Without hesitation, she obeyed. "When I was younger, I loved the word disapprobation. I liked saying it and spelled it whenever and to whomever I could. Meryton, being a small village, offered few who did not know my skill, so I had to find another word that intrigued me. I chose ignoramus. After I wore out my audience, I selected superciliousness." She giggled. "My father called me into his study to inquire how I was choosing my new words. When I explained I had heard

87

them used by some of the ladies about my mother, he told me I had to stop and find some other way of astounding the neighborhood with my intellect."

"How old were you?" They were already six steps down the second set of stairs. Two more and he could relax. *Ha! Impossible!* He would not relax until he was breathing fresh air in daylight or candlelight.

"I was in my eighth year," she boasted.

"I wish I would have known you then." And, he did. How different would he have been to have had a friend of a young Elizabeth instead of Wickham? He shook his head. As she had said, there was no benefit to looking back because nothing could be changed at this time in his life.

She laughed as they went down the last two steps. "You would have been the perfect fodder for my vocabulary, William. At almost eight years older, you would have paid me no attention at all. However, I could have expanded my personal glossary from your ignoring me. Grandiose. Affected. Grandiloquent. Magniloquent. Vainglorious. All perfectly lovely descriptions of an adolescent who was the antithesis of me."

Stretching his hand forward, he touched the rough surface of old books and the hard panel behind. They were at the door.

"Richard!" They heard the colonel as he approached.

"Darcy? Miss Elizabeth?" His cousin pounded on the edge of the bookshelf. Darcy felt the blows under his hands. "How do I open this infernal door?"

"You must listen closely, or you will be trapped inside with us. Do *not* touch anything yet," Darcy commanded. "When you pull the hidden lever, the floor will spin rotating the bookshelf and delivering you into the passage and us back into the library. Do you understand? You will need to pull the switch then jump back out of the way. Do you see where the circular seam is in the floor? Make sure you land behind that mark."

"I understand. Let us get you out of there, Darce."

"Good." Darcy hesitated, then charted his course. "A moment, please?"

Turning, he grabbed for Elizabeth's hand, slowly pulling her close.

"I have yet to tell you this, my lady, but I need you to know this important detail before we walk through that door." Courage filled his chest. "I…I ardently love you with my whole heart and soul. I will be the happiest man on earth when you become my wife, Miss Elizabeth Bennet. I love you truly and cannot wait to welcome you as Mrs. Darcy to our home."

"Oh!"

Taking advantage of her shock, he lowered his mouth to hers.

Heaven. Paradise. Chocolate and good wine. She tasted of the best things in life and his heart fairly burst, not from fear, but from the intense rapture he felt from holding her in his arms.

The pounding from behind him interrupted the best few seconds of his lifetime. He vowed in his heart to make Richard miserable for that same period of time in the near future.

Dropping another quick kiss on her soft lips, he turned back to the door.

"At chest height there is a book you pull back which will release the lever. It is the third one from the edge."

Their rescue was rapidly done. Within seconds, he and Elizabeth spun into the library to be greeted by a smiling Richard Fitzwilliam.

Relief infiltrated every pore in Darcy's body. Gone was the darkness. Instead, they were surrounded by glowing candlelight as both Richard and Smyth held lit torches bright enough to hurt their eyes.

"You both are a sight," was the first thing out of his cousin's mouth.

"Well, hello to you too," smirked Elizabeth.

Nine

DARCY

Lady Catherine de Bourgh stood in the doorway of the room.

"Nephew, what have you done?" As she stalked towards them, he noted her parson trailing her like a shadow. "You have inconvenienced my whole household by your foolishness."

"I was rescuing your guest." Taking deep breaths, calming his throbbing heart, and wiping his palms on the sides of his filthy trousers, he had no time for his aunt's nonsense.

Mrs. Collins, who had followed her husband into the library, embraced Elizabeth as Richard poured the only readily available liquid into two glasses, seeing to their most pressing need.

Gratefully, Darcy held the first gulp of brandy in his mouth, allowing it to wet all the surfaces before swallowing. Elizabeth was doing the same with a much more modest amount.

"We need water for drinking and bathing before we discuss the consequences of our afternoon's activities." Darcy looked directly at his aunt, expecting her acquiescence although anticipating her balking at daring to give a command in her domain.

"We will talk now, Nephew. Mrs. Collins can take her guest home to do with her whatever is her inclination." Lady Catherine arrogantly lifted her nose and turned to leave the room. Over her shoulder she imparted her final words on the subject, "She is wholly unconnected to me and will be the same to you by the time I am done."

Darcy looked to the butler and some of the staff pressing into the doorway. "If you will close the door behind you?" Even to his own ears he heard the voice of authority. He would brook no arguments from anyone. He had one lady, and one lady only, who ruled his heart, and she was standing next to him.

His glare at the room's occupants had immediate effect. Mrs. Collins and her young sister seated themselves on a sofa next to the fireplace. Richard moved to the mantel where his relaxed posture was a ruse. He was as attentive to the group as ever.

Lady Catherine remained in her position, which meant her parson did as well.

At a knock on the door, Darcy called, "This had better be good, Smyth."

It was. In the butler's hands were two large mugs brimming with water. He handed one to Darcy and Elizabeth before, again, departing the room.

Drinking deeply, Darcy sighed as the first drops hit his mouth. As the liquid danced across his tongue, he glanced at Elizabeth. Her eyes closed as she took the first swallow. Suddenly, he no longer thirsted for the mug's contents. He yearned for her. He ached for her.

Turning to his aunt, he announced, "I am pleased to inform you all that Miss Elizabeth Bennet has agreed to be my wife. As she is the future Mistress of Pemberley and Darcy House, I expect her to be treated with the respect due her position. Should you choose not to do so, any association with the Darcy name and family will end, right now."

He turned to his intended. "Will you be recovered from our adventure enough to return to Longbourn on the morrow? I am anxious to speak with your father so our wedding can be arranged."

"But, sir…" Mr. Collins began, his tone offensive in his distaste for the subject being discussed. "Miss Elizabeth has accepted your offer? How can this be?"

"Darcy! How can you?" his aunt demanded her say. "Will you step away from her and…"

The couple ignored them both. Elizabeth gave him her full attention, her lovely eyes never wavering from his.

"I will be ready when you are, William." She spoke so softly he leaned towards her.

Lord, but he wanted to kiss her again.

Instead, he inquired, "Might I escort you back to the parsonage?"

She giggled. "While I thank you for being a dutiful admirer, sir, I see our most pressing need being a good scrubbing. Will I see you once the task is done?"

His joy was so complete, he looked out of the window expecting sunshine and blue skies. Except, the heavy grey clouds continued to release pouring rain.

"My dear, do you not suppose a brisk walk in the weather would clear our lungs and wash away most of the dirt and cobwebs?"

"What an amazingly delightful prospect."

She immediately accepted his extended arm. "If you will pardon us?"

Richard smirked, Mrs. Collins and her sister smiled, and Lady Catherine and her lackey sputtered as Darcy walked Elizabeth out of the room.

***

Stepping from the front covered portico, the raindrops hit them with vigor. Elizabeth tilted her face to the skies and gathered the liquid in her palms.

"Oh, this is wonderful, William. Does it not feel refreshing?"

He adored her smile. He imitated her actions and understood her joy.

Within moments, the curls on his head were plastered to his forehead. He failed to notice as the weight of her tresses were bogged with the water. Reaching up, she pulled out her hairpins, handing them to him. Her braid fell heavily to her waist.

She had left her pelisse and bonnet behind. Instead, she had accepted a shawl from his aunt's housekeeper, which could be easily laundered. For the same reason, he did not wear his greatcoat. The garments they had worn into the passage would only soil anything placed over them.

"This spring shower is cold. Let us hurry." Elizabeth set a brisk pace towards her temporary home. "You are a funny man, William Darcy."

"Me? Never in my lifetime have I been so accused." He laughed. She knew him—really knew the inner man—and he was grateful.

"Ha! Had you chosen to remain behind, I would have run to Charlotte's house. Despite our lack of proper outer clothes, which in itself is highly improper, I cannot make myself run in your presence."

He took off. His long legs burned up the distance.

"No fair!" He heard her steps behind his, her laughter almost drowned out by the drops hitting the ground.

Stopping suddenly, he grabbed her before she could pass, pulling her to him.

Her arms snuck under his coat as she shivered in his embrace.

He rested his head atop hers, catching the drips on the side of his face, shielding her.

"Elizabeth," he spoke quietly, knowing she would adjust her position until her ear was close to his mouth.

He kissed her lobe.

Not wanting her to think it was his only intent, he revealed his heart, "I am free. There is no darkness. The space is wide. Should I choose to move my arms, which I will not, I can reach them as far from me as possible with no possibility of being confined. I am free."

Drawing her head back a mite, she said, "I, too, am free. I am free to place my hand in yours. I am free to run to you for your strength when needed. I am free to share my most secret concerns, and I will never fear anything so long as I have you."

"Then let us move forward with confidence," he insisted.

They took two steps towards the parsonage when a movement on the ground under the shrubs caught the corner of his eye.

Oh, dear Lord, please do not let her see it.

Too late.

Her scream rang out, her feet dancing on the ground as her arms flailed. Her next movement caught him completely by surprise. In a move he had never seen before, she leapt into his arms, her hands tight around his neck and her face buried at his throat.

She had not over-exaggerated her reaction to a garden snake. But, he did not mind. Shifting her weight to better hold her tightly, he whispered for her ears alone, "Do not look, my love, for it was merely a stick on the ground. A small twig, miniscule in size, with no threat to you or to me. No, do not look, Elizabeth, for I do believe it tiny enough you could not push embroidery thread through it should it have a hole at one end. No, Elizabeth, you have no need to look for we have moved away from where the stick lay under the lilac bush. Can you smell the flowers? Even in the rain, are they not fragrant? Why, I do not believe a mighty woman like you could be afraid of an infinitesimally petite shard of wood, do you? No, not my Elizabeth."

Her chuckle tickled the skin above his collar.

"I love you, William."

Her words were music to his ears and almost brought him to his knees. He wanted to keep her with him forever. Where he had once been lost and alone, he was now found and possessed by the woman of his dreams. He had come to Kent a single man of good fortune but would depart on the morrow the happiest of men. *Could life get any better?*

Epilogue

DARCY

One year later –

He had been wrong. The last ten months of marriage to Elizabeth had proved to him he had no clue what true love was. For a certainty, he had been honest in his comments then. However, the reality of his marriage was better than he could have imagined.

Nonetheless, at times, he wanted to pull his hair out as he sought to determine how best to please her. Just when he thought he had the upper hand, she trumped him with a gesture or a comment that reached into his heart and warmed the hard edges until they melted into a puddle at her feet.

Their first night together as man and wife brought him clarity and healing. Mischievously, she pulled the blanket over them as she burrowed next to him, cocooning them in darkness. Unintentionally, the light quilt reached the top of his head, covering his eyes, and blackening everything around him.

Before he could pull the fabric off him, she did.

He had a champion. He no longer needed to fear.

***

They had invited Lady Catherine and Anne to their wedding. Their invitation was ignored by Rosings Park and the parsonage. Not having Mrs. Collins there to share her happiness was a sadness Elizabeth suffered from for weeks.

Yet, when she received her laundered petticoat from Lady Catherine's housekeeper with a note from Charlotte tucked inside, they both laughed at the wonder Mrs. Collins must have had when presented with the cleaned garment. How could its existence in a dark corner of Rosings be explained properly to someone who had not lived the circumstance? It could not be done.

Elizabeth had insisted shortly after they arrived in Pemberley that the existing abandoned mine shafts be filled. When she tenderly explained how one day their sons would roam the estate playing hide and seek as Darcy and Richard had done, he quickly saw to her request.

Now, on the eve of the anniversary of the prior year's visit to Rosings, he waited for Elizabeth to finish dressing for dinner. Georgiana had already joined him in the drawing room as had Richard. They gathered at Pemberley to await the birth of the first Darcy child.

Their party would grow extensively on the morrow as the Bennets and Bingleys, meaning Mr. and Mrs. Charles and Jane Bingley, would be joining them. Bingley's pernicious sisters were not invited.

Darcy looked at the clock on the mantel as it chimed the hour. *Where was Elizabeth?* Normally, she met him at the top of the stairs and they descended together.

The thought had barely crossed his mind when her personal maid entered the room. Approaching him, she kept her voice calm as she admitted, "Sir, I seem to have misplaced Mrs. Darcy. I went into the dressing room to place the jewels she did not choose back in the safe, and when I returned she had vanished. I searched the chambers thoroughly and find no evidence of where she has gone."

Panic, shear terror filled him as he ran from the room to check for himself. He had shown her the three secret passageways and how to enter and exit them the day after she had arrived with him in Derbyshire. They were no longer a threat to either of them as candles and the means to light them had be placed on each end of the narrow halls.

She was, indeed, gone.

Spinning, he gave the room a cursory search, his eyes stopping on the small stocking resting on his pillow. She had been knitting baby garments since she had felt the quickening. His sweetly impatient wife had never quite mastered the task.

What should have been a gown looked more like a sack. What should have been a cap to cover a baby's curls, looked like a bowl. He swore that the last pair of booties she tried to make would have fit him, though he only noted it to himself. She was trying, with her heart going into every stitch.

This tiny stocking looked promising.

He lifted it and weighed it in his hand. He barely felt the yarn, it was so small. Smiling at her accomplishment, his heart calmed. The perspiration which had gathered at the news of her missing dried up. His hands were steady as he checked the design she had included—a pony. Or, was it a puppy? A turtle? For a certainty, it was not a snake.

Chuckling to himself, he walked down the hall to the nursery. He found her there, one hand rhythmically stroking her extended belly and the other on the cradle every Darcy had used for generations.

She was crying.

Stepping behind her, his hands rested over hers.

"My Elizabeth are you well?" He felt when the muscles tightened under the waist that was no longer there.

"I will miss dinner," she admitted.

"As will I."

"I will miss welcoming my family."

"I will welcome them with open arms."

She grinned. "My mother?"

"Yes, Mrs. Bennet as well." Mrs. Bennet was not his favorite of the family, but she had given birth to five healthy children. He thought her encouragement would be of value to Elizabeth.

"I will miss seeing you, as the midwife will banish you from the room."

"Ah, now I understand," he confessed. "You worry I will be lost without you. Well, know this to be a truth, my dearest. I would be lost without you. But once delivered of our child, we will find a happiness we have never imagined. Do you not agree?"

He nuzzled her neck as another sharp pain racked her body.

"Then, it is time, William."

***

Hours later, when he held his son in his arms, he pondered all he had gained by marriage to his wife. The loss of his bachelorhood, the loss of full control over his own life, and the loss of his obligation to return to Rosings in Kent paled with what he had found. In his hands was the greatest gift his wife could have given him, a little one created from bonds of love strong enough to withstand the loss of every material thing should it happen.

Fitzwilliam Darcy had found his one true love. And she had found him. When he lost his heart to her, he found happiness.

The End

From the Author:

Christie Capps is the pen name of a best-selling author J Dawn King who, because of increasing demands on her time, has fewer and fewer hours to read. She doubts she is the only one with these circumstances. Therefore, her Christie Capps stories will all be approximately 100 pages of sweet romance and will be priced less than one cup of flavored coffee from your local barista.

Happy reading!

ALREADY AVAILABLE in eBook, Print, and Audio format

FROM CHRISTIE CAPPS:

Mr. Darcy's Bad Day

For Pemberley

The Perfect Gift

Forever Love

Boxed Set: Something Old, New, Later, True

Elizabeth

Currently, these books are available exclusively at Amazon, CreateSpace, Audible, and iTunes (for audio only). In the near future they will be on all retail markets.

ALREADY AVAILABLE in eBook, Print, and Audio format

FROM J Dawn King:

Friends and Enemies

Mr. Darcy's Mail-Order Bride

Love Letters from Mr. Darcy

The Abominable Mr. Darcy

Yes, Mr. Darcy

Compromised!

One Love, Two Hearts, Three Stories

A Father's Sins

COMING SOON from J Dawn King!

Letter of the Law

Thank you very much for investing your time with this story. A gift for any author is to receive an honest review from readers. I hope you will use this opportunity to let others know your opinion of this tale. Happy reading!

Printed in Great Britain
by Amazon